A Billy and Blaze Book

BLAZE FINDS FORGOTTEN ROADS

BLAZE FINDS FORGOTTEN ROADS

Story and Pictures by C. W. ANDERSON

MACMILLAN PUBLISHING CO., INC.
New York
COLLIER MACMILLAN PUBLISHERS
London

Macmillan Publishing Co., Inc.
866 Third Avenue, New York, N.Y. 10022
Collier Macmillan Canada, Ltd.
ISBN 0-02-701340-5
Library of Congress catalog card number: 76-117970

10 9 8 7 6 5 4

To my granddaughter, Sheila

Billy and Tommy were good friends, and their
ponies, Blaze and Dusty, liked each other too.
The boys took long rides through the woods
and over the hills almost every day.

One day they decided to go exploring. There
were many old roads they had never tried.
Their mothers had packed lunches for them,
and they were excited about their adventure.

As they started out Billy said, "Let's make this a game. We will take every right turn we come to and see what we find."

"Fine!" said Tommy. "That will be fun. We'll see new country."

The first road on the right was overgrown and looked as if it had not been used for a long time. A big twisted tree seemed to be trying to bar their way, but they pushed aside the branches and went on.

The branches were so thick they could barely see the road. "Do you think it leads anywhere?" asked Tommy.

"Somebody must have lived here once," said Billy. "Otherwise there wouldn't be a road."

The branches grew thicker and thicker, and
Billy was just about to turn back when he saw
an open space ahead. They hurried on and
soon came out into the open.

14

In the clearing they saw the ruins of a log
cabin. The walls had fallen, but a stone
fireplace and part of the chimney still stood.

"This must be very old," said Billy. "Look
at the moss on the stones and logs."

They tied their ponies to a tree and went to look at the ruins. In one side of the fireplace was a large, rusty hook.

"That was to hang a pot from," said Billy. "People used to do their cooking that way."

As they were walking around, Billy stubbed his toe on something. He went back to look, then got a sharp stick and began to dig. When he had rubbed the dirt from what he had found, he called to Tommy.

"Look! It's a little powder horn."

As he cleaned it more carefully he saw that a name had been cut in the side of the horn.

"Billy Conroy," he read. "That must have been the boy's name. And he lived here long ago!"

Billy found a piece of string in his pocket and tied it to the powder horn so he could hang the horn from his shoulder. It was nice to have something so old that had once belonged to another Billy.

Tommy was looking around to see what he could find.

Tommy pushed aside dust and plaster on the mantel of the old fireplace.

"I think I've found something!" he called excitedly as he hurried over to Billy.

"It's an Indian arrowhead," said Billy. "I've seen pictures of them, but I've never seen a real one before. You're lucky, Tommy."

Both boys were very happy when they mounted
their ponies and started off.

"Let's follow this trail," said Billy as he
turned off the road. "It looks as if it was used
a long time ago, so it must lead somewhere.
And it turns to the right."

Now the branches were so thick that they had to lie flat on their ponies' backs to get through. Billy had begun to wonder if this overgrown trail really did lead anywhere, when he heard running water.

Soon they came to a clearing where they found a small waterfall and a clear, dark pool. The ponies whinnied and hurried forward to have a drink of the cool water.

Billy and Tommy tied their ponies where they could graze, then sat beside the pool to eat their lunches. They were hungry, and it was peaceful and pleasant.

"Indians probably came here for water long ago. Don't you think so?" said Tommy.

"I'm sure they did," said Billy. "Maybe Indian boys sat right where we are sitting. It's such a nice place."

After lunch they followed another trail to the right. The farther they went the more overgrown it became, and it was hard to see ahead in the dark woods.

At last Billy called Blaze to stop and looked all around. "I can't see any trail at all. Can you, Tommy?"

"No," said Tommy. He was a little frightened, for it was growing late. "Which way shall we go?"

"We'll let Blaze decide," said Billy. "He always knows the way home. Go on, Blaze," he said.

At last they saw a road far off through the
trees.

"You see, Tommy, Blaze did know the way."
Billy patted Blaze and they started toward
the road.

When they were almost out of the woods Billy saw a stream with steep banks ahead of them. He looked around but there was no other way to go.

"We'll have to jump," said Billy. "Do you think Dusty will do it?"

"Yes," said Tommy. "He'll try anything that Blaze does."

"Follow me!" called Billy, and as Blaze sailed over the stream he could hear Dusty right behind them. When he heard Tommy call out "Good boy, Dusty!" he knew they were over.

When they came out on the road, Blaze turned right. It was dusk, and Billy was growing a little worried. An owl hooted, and it sounded scary in the dark woods. Then Billy saw another road ahead with a stone wall on each side of it. He knew that road!

"We're near home, Tommy," he called out. "We'll be home before it's really dark."

They went along at a gallop now, and they
were very happy. Exploring had been fun, and
both Billy and Tommy had found something
from long ago that they would always keep.
It had been an exciting day.